# MY SNAKE Blake

RANDY SiEGEL • SeRGE BLOCh

A NEAL PORTER BOOK
ROARING BROOK PRESS
NEW YORK

I was in my room,
hiding from my homework,
when my dad knocked on the door,
handed me a big box with a red ribbon on top,
and shouted:

"Happy Early Birthday!"

"Hurry up and open it."

"C'mon! It needs air."

This made me quite curious.

So I ripped off the wrapping paper,
tore open the box,
and yelled, "Oh Wow!"
Because inside was a cage
with a super-long, bright green snake inside.
"I can't believe you got me a snake!" I said.
"You'd better believe it," said my dad.

"I think your father is nuts," said my mom,
as she walked in, frowning.
"And proud of it," answered my dad.
"Now let the snake out."

"No way!" screeched my mom.

"Yes way!" declared my dad, before adding: "This snake has the right to life, liberty, and the pursuit of happiness."

"Says who?" asked my mom.

"Declaration of Independence, second paragraph," said my dad, snapping his fingers to prove a point.

As I slid open the cage door,
causing my mom to shriek
and jump up on my bed,

the snake stuck out his head,
crawled slowly onto the floor,
slithered around,
and twisted his body into neat, little letters
that spelled:

"He can write!" I gasped.

"Pretty cool, eh?" chuckled Dad. "I paid extra for that."

"Awesome," I said. "What should I call him?"

"Why don't you ask him?" said Dad.

So I did.

he wrote after squirming for a second.

"What sort of name is Blake for a snake?" I asked.

"Beats me," said Dad.

"Well, if that's what he wants, then that's what he gets," I said.

"Yeah, we better not make Blake mad," said Mom. "He might bite."

Blake gave her a dirty look and rolled around.

he scribbled.

"Really?" said Mom.

he answered.

Sure enough,
to this day,
Blake has never bitten anyone.
Or gotten mad.
Or done anything bad.
He's been a perfectly polite, delightful snake,
as even my mom has discovered.

Blake can cook like a great chef,
even though he likes to lick the dishes clean
instead of using the dishwasher.

He catches flies,

and can find pretty much
anything,
including car keys

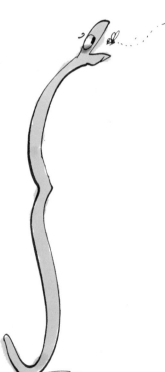

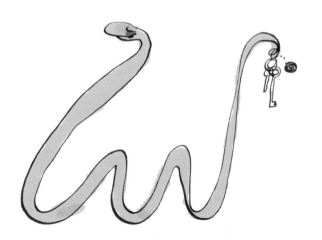

and remote control clickers
for the TV.

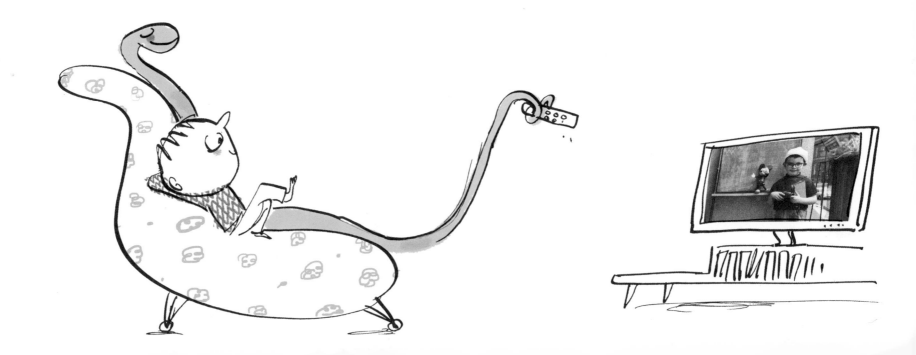

Best of all, Blake is always there to help me do my homework,

even when I'd rather be doing something else.

Whenever I get to a tough question,
Blake has the answer.

"When was bubble gum invented?"
"1906."

How much is 987 + 327 x 63 ÷ 6?
"13,797."

"What is the capital of Kenya?"
"Nairobi."

Who was the Oakland Raiders' quarterback
when they won the Super Bowl in 1977?

*"Kenny 'The Snake' Stabler."*

Which British poet wrote
*Songs of Innocence and of Experience?*

*"Blake,"* he wrote, and smiled.

And whenever I have a problem,
Blake helps me solve it.

Like the time my parents
made me eat Brussels sprouts
at dinner,
and Blake ate them
after I dropped them (on purpose)
under the table.

Or the time that kid Kevin
was mean to me at school,
and Blake stuck his tongue out and hissed.

Or whenever I'm running late to catch the school bus and don't have time to walk the dog.

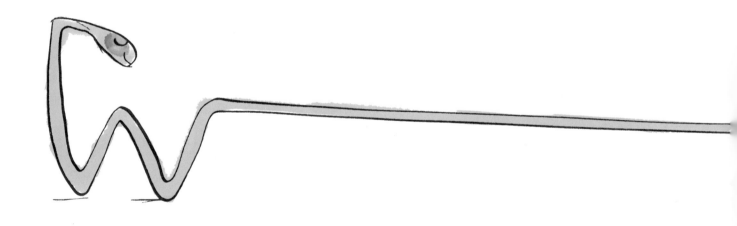

And yes, from time to time,
whenever Blake has a problem,
I'm there for him, too.

Like when our family flew on a plane to Florida,
and several passengers—plus a poodle—got VERY upset.

I realize that dogs, cats, and horses
have been, are, and always will be,
the most popular pets,
getting tons and tons of love and attention.

But I'm lucky to have my snake, Blake,
who is the best snake, by far,
in the whole wide world.

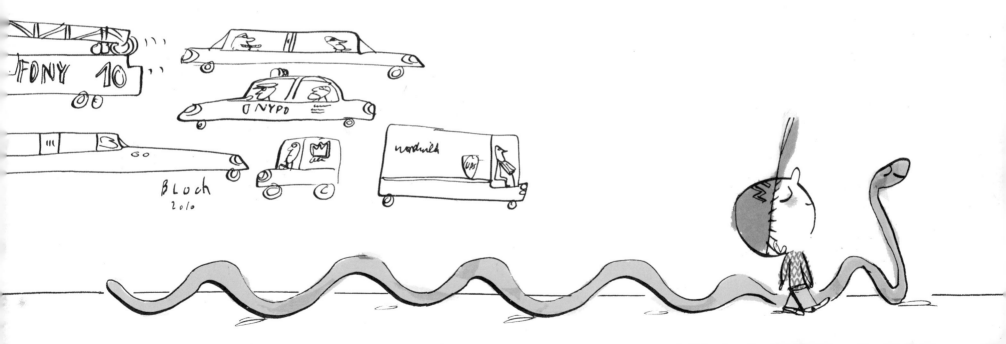

*To Lisa for her love*
*and Austin for his love of reptiles.* —R.S.

Text copyright © 2012 by Randy Siegel   Illustrations copyright © 2012 by Serge Bloch

A Neal Porter Book   Published by Roaring Brook Press

Roaring Brook Press is a division of Holtzbrinck Publishing Holdings Limited Partnership

175 Fifth Avenue, New York, New York 10010

mackids.com

Library of Congress Cataloging-in-Publication Data

Siegel, Randy.

    My snake Blake / Randy Siegel ; illustrations by Serge Bloch. — 1st ed.

       p. cm.

    "A Neal Porter Book."

    Summary: The extremely long, bright green snake a boy receives from his
father as an early birthday present proves to be incredibly smart and talented.

    ISBN 978-1-59643-584-1

    [1. Snakes as pets—Fiction. 2. Human-animal relationships—Fiction.] I.
Bloch, Serge, ill. II. Title.

    PZ7.S57545My 2012

    [E]—dc23

                                                                    2011018402

Roaring Brook Press books are available for special promotions and premiums.
For details contact: Director of Special Markets, Holtzbrinck Publishers.

First edition 2012   Book design by Jennifer Browne

Printed in China by South China Printing Company Ltd., Dongguan City, Guangdong Province

10  9  8  7  6  5  4  3  2  1